W9-BKF-401
E LA
Little things
10004406
PROPERTY OF
SCHOOLS
Purchased with PL 864 NDEA Funds
ESEA 19 79
Title IV

LITTLE THINGS

OTHER TALES ILLUSTRATED BY MARCIA SEWALL

Best wishes! Marcia Sewall

The Squire's Bride
by P. C. Asborjnsen

Coo My Dove, My Dear
by Joseph Jacobs

LITTLE THINGS

by ANNE LAURIN

illustrated by Marcia Sewall

ATHENEUM 1978 NEW YORK

Library of Congress Cataloging in Publication Data

Laurin, Anne. Little things.

SUMMARY: A man amiably accustoms himself to
the inconveniences presented by his wife's ever growing
blanket until he finds that he will have to accustom
himself to losing his wife.
I. Sewall, Marcia. II. Title.
PZ7.L372794Li [E] 77-23868
ISBN 0-689-30623-7

Published simultaneously in Canada by
McClelland & Stewart, Ltd.
Manufactured in the United States of America by
The Book Press, Brattleboro, Vermont
First Edition

For Linda B. & Peter B.

The days were turning colder and darker when Mrs. B. decided to knit a blanket for her husband and herself. She sat down in the rocking chair in the far corner of her living room and began.

That night when Mr. B. came in from planting the winter crop, Mrs. B. had already completed a fine square of blanket.

"Dear," Mr. B. asked, "what are you doing?"

"I'm knitting a blanket for these cold winter nights," Mrs. B. answered and continued her knitting.

"That's lovely," Mr. B. said, and he left her alone to work. He never bothered her when she was working, and although he was very hungry, he would wait for dinner. Little things like waiting for dinner never upset Mr. B.

Never.

When Mr. B. got out of bed in the morning, he found Mrs. B. still knitting in the living room.

"Mrs. B., dear," he said. "Didn't you come to bed last night?"

"No," Mrs. B. answered without raising her eyes from her work. "I simply must finish this blanket before the snow falls."

And though Mr. B. was still hungry from missing dinner, he decided to wait for breakfast until lunch. Breakfast was such a little thing, and little things never upset Mr. B.

But at noon there was no lunch, so Mr. B. decided to wait for breakfast and lunch until dinner. And when there was no dinner for dinner, Mr. B. decided to make his own.

"Dearest," Mr. B. said to Mrs. B., "I have made something to eat. Would you care to join me?"

"No, no," Mrs. B. answered, "I've work to do."

So Mr. B. ate alone and went to bed.

The next morning, after Mr. B. had made himself some breakfast, he found that Mrs. B.'s blanket now filled the entire living room, and he could only just see her in the far corner, fast at work.

"Dear Mrs. B.," he said, "I see that your fine square of a blanket has grown into a fine room of a blanket."

"Thank you," she answered without missing a stitch.

He blew her a kiss and went off to the fields. Little things like not being able to go into his living room didn't bother Mr. B.

And so it went, as Mr. B. worked the farm and made his meals and slept, Mrs. B. knitted and knitted and knitted. Mr. B. didn't mind when the blanket crept into the kitchen or down the hall or into the bedroom.

"How convenient that I can use the blanket on my own bed while my wife works on it," he thought.

He became a little worried when he could no longer find the bed, because all he *could* find was Mrs. B.'s blanket. But then he thought, "Well, how convenient. I don't need a bed anymore. I can curl up on this blanket anywhere."

And he did.

One day several of his neighbors came to call. They had to shout from the road because by now Mrs. B.'s blanket had eased out the doors and windows, over the porch and all around the house.

"Good day," Mr. B. said when he finally got to them.

"Good day," one of his neighbors said. "Your wife has gone and made a blanket that fills your entire house."

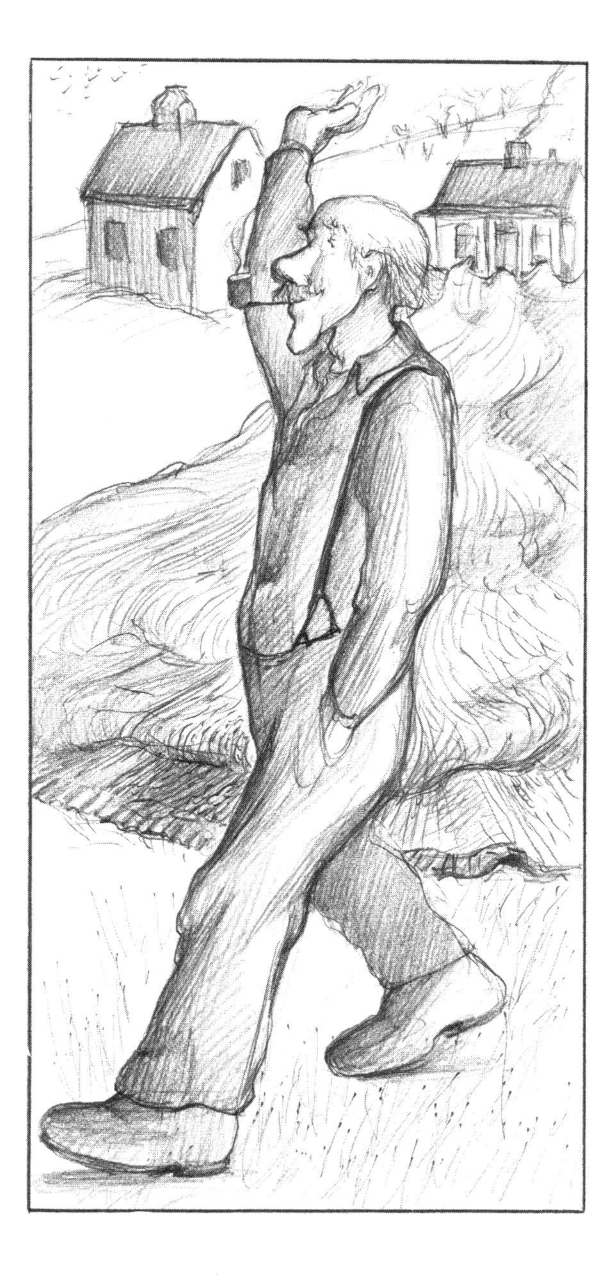

"And some of it even comes outside," Mr. B. added, smiling.

"Doesn't it bother you?" another neighbor asked.

"No, no, no," Mr. B. said smiling, "little things never bother me."

So Mrs. B.'s blanket moved over the flower garden and down the hill, through the barn and covered the mill. When he went out, one morning, it took Mr. B. half a day just to find his house again. He had to walk carefully over bumps of blanket, lumps where his tractor sat and where his hammock hung. He crawled through his kitchen window and looked around. But he couldn't find Mrs. B. All he could see was folds and mounds and mountains of blanket.

"And where is my precious dear?" Mr. B. called out sweetly. But no one replied.

"Pumpkin?" he said a little louder.

"Lovely!" he called, getting red in the face.

Not to have dinner was all right, and not to have a bed was all right. Even not to have a farm was all right. But now Mr. B. didn't have a wife, either.

"I'll have no more of this," Mr. B. cried. "Would you please, PLEASE stop knitting this blanket."

Mrs. B. dropped her knitting needles and stood up quickly, for she had never heard Mr. B. yell before.

"What's wrong?" she asked.

"Your blanket," Mr. B. said, pointing around him. "It covers the yard and the dog and the cat. And it bothers me."

"Why, dear," Mrs. B. said, still surprised, "little things don't usually bother you."

"But lovely," Mr. B. answered, "your blanket has become such a BIG thing."

Mrs. B. looked around, and as far as she could see there was blanket and blanket and blanket. "My, my," she said, smiling, "it *is* quite large. I hadn't realized. But I think we could cut it up into little blankets and give one or two to each of our neighbors and still have enough to last us many a winter."

And that's what they did.

After they gave a blanket to everyone they knew, and a few people they didn't, they stacked the rest outside the back door. The pile of little blankets went so high that you could barely see the top, and Mr. B. had to walk around it every morning, making sure not to knock it over.

But, you know, the little things never bothered him.

5.91

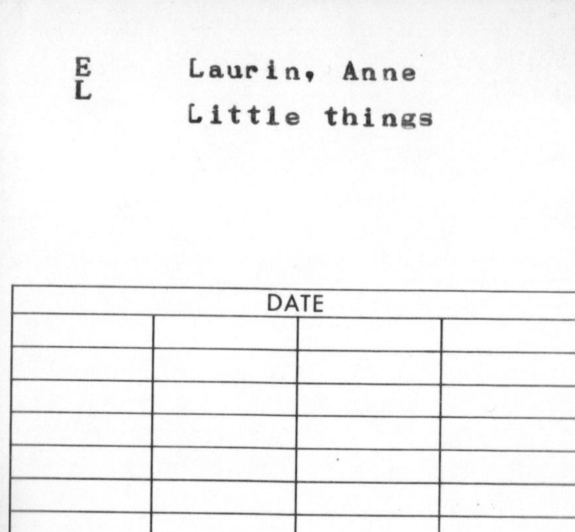